Gypsy Moon

Dahlia Rose

Gypsy Moon
By Dahlia Rose
Copyright © February 2015 Dahlia Rose Unscripted
Cover Art by EDH Graphics

Chapter One

July 5, 1995

The wind was warm against her skin as it blew through the oak tree she lay under. The happy giggles of her sisters filtered through the air as they played down the hills chasing butterflies. Even though it was summer, the weather was surprisingly cool for July. The city had fireworks for the holiday the day before, and they had watched from the hill where she now lay. Life was perfect there.

Her grandmother hummed next to her while she placed each tarot card on the red and white checkered blanket they were on. This was her place, at her grandmother's farm in Kansas. Nadira felt at peace here, but back in the city of Baltimore the apartment she shared *with her mom, stepfather, and sister was always filled with chaos.*

Her stepfather hit her mother and never missed an opportunity to try to grab Nadira's breast or ass since she turned sixteen. She was always scared when her mom was at work. She knew he would take the next step and try to do something, and he was so big she could never fight him off. Her grandmother had given her some good news, though. She and her younger sisters would be moving in with her by the end of the summer. Her grandmother had won full custody from her mother, and she would no longer have to live in fear or watch the abuse her mother took while refusing to leave.

"I've decided, Gran," Nadira announced.

"What's that, sugar bear?" Her grandmother used the pet name she grew up hearing and loving.

"I'm never going to fall in love or get married. I'm going to study hard and get good grades and get a scholarship to music school for the piano," Nadira declared vehemently. "Love hurts. Momma's bruises prove it. I never want that!"

"Don't say that, Nadira," her Gran scolded. "What your mom has is not love. It's cruel and twisted. When love finds you, it makes your heart beat faster, and your tummy does flip flops. It's the greatest feeling in the world. I had it with your grandfather." Her grandmother smiled wistfully as she remembered. "That was my true love, and yours will find you, too."

"Well, I don't want it," she said in a huff. "'If he comes along, I'll send him packing."

Her grandmother laughed. "I'm reading your cards now, sugar bear. There'll be someone, and you won't be able to deny him. Strong, with eyes the color of the deep blue sea. He will be dressed neat and standing tall. When he kisses you, you'll know he's the one, and he will know it, too."

"I don't believe that, Gran. I choose to make my own destiny, my own fate." Nadira glanced up at the sky through the trees.

"No matter how much we try to make fate bend to our will, she is her own master." A strange smile played on her grandmother's lips. "You just watch what happens."

Present Day...

Nadira's fingers moved lightly over the ivory piano keys. The soft drum beat and horn blended in with the mellow saxophone. It created a sensual rhythm that all the couples on the dance floor swayed to in each other's arms. Her band was playing the Military Valentine's ball at Fort Leavenworth, and they were doing it for free.

With all these men and women gave up for their country, Nadira refused to take one penny from them as coordinator for the event. It was the least they could do. Red and white streamers of cut out cupids and red and silver hearts hung down from the ceiling on silver string. Even the napkins represented the day of love that was a week away.

Nadira didn't subscribe to the day of love, but she had to admit whoever decorated went all out. The set ended, and the couples stopped dancing to clap. She almost felt sorry seeing them unlock from their loving embraces. Some people were meant to be in love.

She could see it on each of their faces as they stared at each other, or catch it in a caress that lingered on a cheek. It was for them, not for her, because even at twenty-eight, she had kept the vow to never fall in love. Men friends came and went, but she never let them get close, and she planned to keep it that way.

Nadira spoke into the microphone that was perched on her piano. "This next song is a special piece of music I wrote when I heard I was going to be playing for you guys. You're so brave for doing what you do, and your wives are just as strong for letting you go and keeping everything together until you get back. This is for you, so hold each other tight again. Remember how it felt when you first met."

She closed her eyes and let the music fill her until she could see it in her mind. Her fingers moved by instinct, because she knew each key and note by heart, even though the piece was only created a week ago. The piano was her lover and her best friend. She never felt more at home or loved than when she sat in front of the smooth mahogany.

The music spoke of falling in love and feeling loss when their loved ones went away to war. It spoke of triumphs and new birth, and each key was a memory to be shared over the long distance. It spoke of the re-union of lovers coming together once more.

Nadira slowly opened her eyes and looked out to the crowd. Everyone was dancing—all except one. He stood in the back of the room, and his eyes were on her, nothing else, only her. A deep blue gaze that spoke volumes without speaking a word was set in a ruggedly handsome face with a clean shaven jaw. His lips held just the hint of a smile, and even from the stage where she sat she could tell he was over six feet tall. In his uniform, he looked powerful, and medals adorned his chest

Her breath caught as a sense of knowing flowed over her, and as she played, her grandmother's words came back to her memory. "Fate is her own master. When you see him, you will know, and so will he." She pulled her gaze away from his, refusing to look back as she finished the piece. She felt a tumble in her stomach, like a thousand butterflies were trying to break free.

The music finished, and she excused herself and the band for a short break while couples went back to their seats. The other members of the band went outside to smoke, and she crossed the ballroom to find a seat. He mirrored every footstep she took, following her until only a few steps separated them when she got to an empty table. They stood staring at each other for what seemed like endless minutes until he spoke.

"You're very talented," he said. His voice was deep, smooth, and husky, and she felt as if he was touching her with words alone.

"I should be. I've been playing the piano since I was nine," Nadira replied.

"Years don't make talent. People can play the music flawlessly with no emotion. Each note you play is filled with it." His smile traveled to his eyes. "You're talent-ed."

"I could be cocky." She couldn't help but tease.

"Somehow I doubt it." He held out his hand to her. "Major Logan Ross, United States Army."

Nadira shook his hand, and from the time his hand's grasp enclosed hers, it sent tingles up her arm. "Nadira Webb, pianist."

"I think I want to get to know you, Nadira Webb. I know it for a fact," Logan said.

"Kind of hard. I'm working right now," she replied.

"Let me wait around, and I'll take you out for coffee after," he said.

"You might be some kind of whacko."

"I'll give your band members my information so you feel safe."

"You don't need to. I have a tazer in my purse."

"Well then, I'll make sure I am on my best behavior and still give them my info." Logan smiled, and she couldn't help but return it. "Say yes, Nadira Webb."

Even though her mind screamed no, different words came to her lips. "Yes."

"Good. I'll wait for you right here." Logan sat down.

"This could be a very bad idea," she murmured to herself as she moved across the shiny hardwood floor.

She rejoined her band mates who had come back in from their cigarette break. She picked up the glass from the coaster on her piano and took a long drink of the cool water before sitting again and roaming her fingers across the keys. Unable to resist, she looked over to where she had left him.

He raised his glass in her direction with a smile, and Nadira swallowed nervously. *Stop behaving like a teenager with a crush!* she chided herself. She wasn't going to let one man cause her to lose her cool. It never happened before, and she was not going to let it happen now.

The rest of the night, she could feel his gaze on her as she played. She tried to block him out, but even in the big ballroom his presence was overwhelming. The last song of the night was the one where she sang the sexy lyrics to the music she wrote.

She almost wished she could get away without singing the words. All of a sudden it felt so personal, as if he could see into her soul. She closed her eyes and let the music carry her off like it always did, and even there she was aware of Logan.

"Dreams scatter to the winds, but memories of you will never fade. No, oh no, my darling, they never fade."

The final word was whispered, and it trailed off with the last note of the piano. Applause brought her out of her reverie. She opened her eyes and smiled at the crowd who whistled and cheered. It all faded when she met the intensity of Logan's eyes. His look spoke volumes. He sat patiently while people came up to talk to her and the band packed up for the night.

She saw him walk over to Steve, the bass guitarist, and Logan handed him a card. Steve looked down at the piece of paper in his hand before his gaze went to her with a question in his eyes. Nadira nodded. That was all that was needed. Even though they all played together, she and the rest of the men rarely associated outside of practice and planned events.

They all had lives they kept separate from the music and used the band as an outlet of release. She didn't know what work Steve did or if Jimmy had a wife and child. They all wanted anonymity, and she did as well. The music was the only constant in her life that really meant anything to her.

While she got her music sheets together and the band discussed practices that fit their entire schedule for the coming weeks, she noticed that Logan slipped out. She almost had a sense of relief in thinking he was gone and was surprised to feel disappointment that their meeting might not take place.

"You sure you don't want us to walk you to your car?" Steve asked.

Logan walked back in carrying two tall Styrofoam cups in his hand. "I'll make sure she gets home safe."

Steve gave her a thumbs up before he stepped outside. The door to the ballroom closed with a wooden thump, signaling that she was now very much alone with Major Logan Ross.

He sat in the chair across from her before handing one of the cups. "I figured you might be a Dark Cherry Mocha kind of woman."

She smiled and teased. "You figured correctly."

"Good. I have this all planned out in my head, you know." Logan took a sip from his own cup.

"You have a plan for what, exactly?"

"How I'm going to woo and win you," Logan said simply.

"Really?" she said wryly.

He nodded, his face solemn. "First is coffee and conversation. Next will be dinner where I sweep you off your feet with my charm. I estimate in about six months we'll be happily married with twins on the way."

She almost choked on her mocha. "You're not pulling any punches, are you?"

"None whatsoever," Logan answered. "Honestly, I never do anything like this. Work has taken first priority in my life for a long time. But I saw you and couldn't help it. I just knew."

"You knew what?" she asked, amazed at how breathless her voice sounded all of a sudden.

"That you're the one." His tone was solemn.

"Man, they said you soldiers moved fast," Nadira teased, trying to lighten the mood.

"Maybe they're right, but I'm not doing it because I'm a soldier."

"Why then?"

"Because I know." Logan changed the subject. "So, you've been playing the piano since you were nine. Your family must be very proud."

"I wouldn't know. The only person who mattered isn't around anymore," Nadira said.

"No family?" he asked.

"Oh, I have a mom somewhere. She liked her boyfriend's fist more than her daughters. I have twin sisters two years younger than I am who took off for California to get a singing career. When I contacted them, well, we don't see eye to eye on things most of the time . We have different memories of growing up, it seems, and they told me they were changing the phone number." Nadira sighed. "The only person was my grandmother. She had a farm, and I loved it there. She died three years ago, and since then it's been just me."

He covered her hand with his. "Sometimes people aren't the best thing for your life regardless if they are blood or not."

Nadira gave a soft laugh and pressed the hand he just touched against her heart. "I don't know why I told you any of that."

"I'm your soul mate."

"You're cocky."

"I'm right."

"Uh-huh." Nadira stood and walked over to the short steps that led to the stage. She sat on the bench and lifted the lid to the piano before calling him over with a finger. "Come over here."

Logan covered the small space easily, and instead of taking the steps, he jumped on stage from the front. Even in his dress blues he moved with the ease. "I've never played a note on anything remotely musical."

She didn't know why the urge to share with the man was so great as she ran her fingers over the keys. Or why she couldn't resist him. Logan unbuttoned his uniform coat and laid it on the bench next to him. Nadira watched him with a sidelong glance. She could see the muscles of his defined arms beneath his neatly starched shirt.

Nadira took his big hand in hers to place it on the piano keys. There was such a connection with him, something so deep that she couldn't help but gasp when his fingers twined with hers. Nadira looked at him, wondering if he felt the connection too. When his gaze met hers, a small smile graced his lips. She knew he did.

She opened his hand and traced the line that went from between his thumb and forefinger to the edge of his palm close to the wrist. "You have a long life line."

"You read palms?" he teased.

Nadira gave a husky laugh. "My grandmother would say we are from a long line of gypsies."

"You didn't believe her?" Logan asked.

"She knew things and read tarot. Who knows."

Logan bent his head close to hers. "Since I have this long life, are you in there with me?"

"It doesn't work that way, Major Logan Ross," she teased. "My grandma would tan your hide for making fun of the fates."

"I am by no means making fun of fate. I think it sent me here to you. I wasn't even going to come to this thing, but for some reason. Here I was, all dressed up and alone, waiting for you," he answered solemnly.

Not knowing how to respond, she turned her attention back to the piano. She placed his hand on two of the smooth pieces of ivory. "You keep pressing these two, and we'll make music together."

"I have no doubt that we will." The look of intensity and desire in his eyes was undeniable.

On her side of the piano, she began to play a soulful tune, something she was working on, a piece that wasn't even completed. Somehow, sitting close to him seemed perfect. She nodded, and he pressed the two notes that she instructed him to. The deep tones mixed with what she was playing. Two sides of the same coin, male and female, passion and lust.

The piece spoke of mates, and even though he played only a pair of notes, it made the music complete. The music seemed to affect him in a way that was a total surprise to her. Without preamble he pulled her into his arms and took her lips in a swift kiss, silencing the music and wiping every thought from her head.

Nadira clung to his wide shoulders as his tongue delved deep into her mouth, tasting and inviting her to play. She followed suit, tasting the caramel latte he had been drinking, mixed with his own personal flavor. He was as intoxicating as if she was drinking wine.

She reveled in his lips pressed against her hard, demanding more from one kiss than she ever thought possible. He pulled away suddenly. She stared up at him and saw so much emotion and blatant desire in one hot look.

"This is right," he whispered. Logan rubbed his finger over her full lips. "It scares me how much I want you already, and I just met you. But nothing feels more right."

Nadira nodded. "I feel the same way."

She was never one to give in to impulse. Nadira thought everything through carefully and always had a plan B. Her love life was carefully controlled. No one ever slept over. She never gave more than she was willing, and her heart was always closed off. None of that would work with Logan. Already she was more exposed to him than to anyone in her life. Running on instinct, passion, and desire, she stood, and with trembling fingers slipped the thin strap of her red dress off her shoulders.

This could break your heart, her mind whispered frantically. But she pushed the warning thought away. She watched his eyes darken as she exposed her ebony skin to him in inches as the wispy dress fell from her body.

She repeated his words and stepped into his arms. "This is right."

Logan's lips met hers in a frenzied kiss, while his hands tore at the buttons of his shirt. Her frantic fingers pulled the tie he wore from its perfect knot, and she dropped it to the floor. He pulled her close, and the heated skin of his body made her gasp.

These sensations would be imprinted into her soul forever—the salty taste of his skin when she pressed an open-mouth kiss on his shoulder, the musky oak scent of his aftershave, and his every touch while he molded her to him.

"What are you doing to me?" she wondered out loud. "I've never done... never had anything like this happen in my life."

"Oh, you are intoxicating," he said kissing against the curve of her neck. He looked up at her suddenly. "I will never be able to get enough of you."

His words were a promise of the pleasure to come. Would this last forever? She didn't know, but Nadira decided to focus on tonight and being with him for this one instant in time.

"I want your cock in my mouth," she said, and he groaned in response. He stood, and his fingers and hers fumbled with his shiny belt buckle before sending his pants and boxers down his legs. Logan kicked off his shoes easily and stood naked and proud in front of her while she was on her knees.

Logan's engorged cock jutted erect and thick in front of her, and Nadira didn't hesitate to take the appendage in her mouth. His body strained against her lips, and he grabbed her hair to push himself deeper into her mouth. Nadira took every inch of him, moaning gently as she loved him with her mouth and tongue.

She could taste the salt of his pre-come on the tip when she swirled her tongue over the distended crown. He was long and thick, and she couldn't take him fully into her mouth. With every caress of her mouth on his cock, he made a guttural moan that fueled her need.

"No more." His voice was harsh with need. "It's my turn."

Logan stepped away from her and helped her to her feet. It was him who was now on his knees pulling the tiny scrap of lacy panties down smooth legs. He pulled the cover down over the keys before lifting her to sit on the piano. Her legs were braced on either side of him. The heels of her stilettos were pressed against the dark wooden bench of the baby grand.

Nadira's breath came in tiny pants of anticipation as he looked at her. She watched as he ran one long finger down the slit of her pussy. His gaze never left her as he penetrated her with the digit. Nadira bit back the cry that rose to her lips but couldn't help raising her hips to meet his hand. When he buried his face between her thighs to taste her, she was lost.

Oh sweet Jesus! The thought flashed through her mind when she felt his tongue penetrate her wet snatch. His lips sucked on her clit, and his fingers pressed and spread the soft folds of her flesh. Nadira could hardly stand it. She moaned as the sensations rolled through from his expert tongue and flooded her senses.

He drove her beyond reason, and all she wanted to feel was his cock fucking her. His tongue never stopped its ministrations until she came hard against his mouth, crying out his name and holding onto his head. He stood so quickly the bench scraped across the stage and fell over. He held her legs around his waist, and she felt the head of his cock at the entrance of her pussy before he filled her.

Logan's hands cupped her ass tight while he thrust himself inside to the hilt. She felt the cool surface of the piano on her back while he pumped into her. He gave a harsh moan before bending low and taking her nipple into his mouth.

"Oh God, Logan, more. Please take it all!" she cried out in earnest.

"Yes, give it all over to me, darling. Let me feel you take me all in," he muttered against her breasts. "God, you feel like liquid heat around me. Open your eyes. I want to see what I do to you. I want to see the pleasure." Logan's voice was a harsh passionate command. "Open your eyes!"

She opened her eyes and saw the vivid darker blue of his eyes aroused with passion. Nadira reached up with tenderness and cupped his cheek for an instant in the midst of all the sexual yearning around them. He thrust into her harder, and her body began to shudder beneath him.

"Come for me, baby," Logan said between gritted teeth.

She could see him straining to hold onto the last vestige of control while he drove her to a blinding orgasm that made her scream and clutch at his shoulders. He never stopped his thrusts into her pussy. Instead, her orgasm seemed to spur him on. She could feel Logan's body tense and shudder before she exploded and shattered in ecstasy once more.

Nadira never knew gratification like this. She hardly caught a breath. Logan watched her tumble off that pleasurable edge. He slid deep into her wet pussy, and his hot come spilled inside her. Together they lay against the piano trying to catch their breath, and Nadira tried to comprehend how she came to be in this place with this man.

Logan looked down at her and smiled then brushed her cheek with a gentle kiss. "Come home with me."

She smiled. "I have a rule that I never have sleep-overs."

"I'm not one for following rules, love." He kissed her again, and she felt his cock jump inside her. "But I don't mind wooing my girl. My daddy made sure to show me how."

"This is wooing?" Nadira teased. "I think we skipped a few steps. We're having a conversation in a rather compromising position if you haven't noticed."

Logan strode the short distance to where the bench tilted over and put it in an upright position. He returned to where she waited in anticipation and lifted her into his arms. When he took her back to the bench, he sat on it and positioned her to straddle his lap, making sure his cock was buried in her center once more. She moaned when she felt him deep inside her, marveling at how he could still be hard.

"We can take it slow or so you may think we are. I'll take you on dates, to the movies, to dinner, and for long walks by the lake," he informed her. "But come Valentine's Day, you'll be mine, even if we skipped a few initial steps."

"Like I said, you're cocky. No pun intended." Nadira couldn't help but smile. He was so sure of himself, and that scared her all the more.

"Oh, I intend to use this to my advantage." He flexed his hips, and the movements sent his cock deeper inside her. "I want more of you already. You're so damn beautiful, naked and dressed."

He took her lips in a searing kiss. *I'm still wearing my heels,* she thought vaguely before his touch wiped all thought from her mind again.

Chapter Two

Logan drove her home, and all the way he had a silly smile on his face. He went to the military ball because there had to be at least one ranking officer on hand to chaperone. He didn't know why. These were men in the middle of a war, who were longing to get home.

The only thing they were interested in was holding their wives or husbands tight and forgetting they were gone for months at a time. This time he definitely couldn't grumble about his duties, because it had given him the opportunity to meet Nadira.

While he drove, the moon caught his attention. It was huge, hanging low in the sky, even though it wasn't quite full. "That's some sight. The moon looks like you could reach out and touch it."

"Gran called it the gypsy moon when she saw it like this," Nadira said. "Every few years it looks like that for a few days, and on Valentine's Day, it will be a full moon. She said beneath it people fall in love."

Logan smiled. "I like your grandmother's stories."

"That's all they were—stories," Nadira replied bluntly. "We all know life does not turn out that way."

She was amazing in all facets, even though she was jaded in a way. From the time he saw her on the stage looking all put together in the slinky red dress she was wearing, he wanted to ruffle that polished exterior. Her eyes were smoke. She'd sung as if just for him, and when he tasted her and loved her, he knew it was the truth.

Nadira sat next to him with her hair just a little bit tousled after their lovemaking. The thought of her creamy dark skin, the way she gasped his name or begged him for more, made him shift in his seat with arousal. Her full lips alone made him want to pull the car over and kiss her until he was sated. But beneath all that, he could see her vulnerability.

Those brown, almond shaped eyes held a hint of sadness. Her past played a key role in how she lived her life. Logan knew he would have to take it slow, even though in their first meeting they combusted together like putting a match to gasoline.

"My apartment is over here." She pointed to the corner where a large building with balconies faced the street.

He pulled into the gate. The complex reminded him of a converted, old style fort. "This is a nice place."

"I'm updating my grandmother's house to move back out there. So this is home for now." She laughed self-consciously. "Why am I telling you my life again?"

"Because we're getting to know each other," Logan said. "I'll even help you with the home renovations if you let me."

"Are you good with swinging a hammer?" Nadira raised a perfectly manicured eyebrow at him.

"I'm good with my hands. I thought I just proved that," Logan teased. He pulled into the parking spot next to the building that she pointed out. "You want me to come in and check under the bed for monsters?"

Nadira unlocked her belt buckle and turned in the seat to face him. "I stopped believing in monsters a long time ago. The real life ones are scary enough. Slow and steady, Logan, let's take the steps, okay?"

Logan nodded and leaned in for a kiss when she caressed his cheek. Her kisses made him crave more, but he sat in his seat and watched her leave the car and unlock the door to her townhouse apartment. When she was safely inside, he left the complex, marveling at his fortune. He couldn't deny her the request. He could already see it in her, in her eyes, the urge to run.

He had known her less than a night, but the signs were in the nervous way she plucked at her dress on the drive home or the way she checked him out from beneath a hooded gaze when she thought he was concentrating on driving. He was someone she couldn't control, a relationship that was not on her terms, and it scared the crap out of her.

Good, Logan thought. He wanted to keep her constantly on her toes, because it would be the only way he would win her heart. Logan decided from the time her husky voice said yes that he was not going to let her go. God, her voice alone made him think of satin sheets and licking caramel off her ebony skin. Nadira made him think of home and hearth.

He had waited a long time to feel that. He pulled into his base housing, a small house that was the exact replica of all the others in that area. He would never bring a family here to live, where you couldn't really spread out and grow. He could see himself with horses and children running and playing on the land around the house. The figure next to him was no longer faceless. It was Nadira.

Inside he built a fire in the small fireplace before gabbing a cold Michelob amber from the fridge. He sat on the leather couch that was way too big for the small living room, but he refused to give up. Logan had a smile on his face when he began to plan his seduction of Nadira. The chase was on, and he loved a good chase.

MORNING CAME FILTERING in through a crease in her drapes. She turned, and the sliver of the sun rays hit her directly in her eyes. Nadira winced and shied away from the offensive glare and covered her head with the blanket with a groan. She sat up and looked at the time.

Eight thirty a.m. Great. Sighing, she threw the blankets aside and got up from bed. Even though she got in at three a.m. she wouldn't be able to go back to sleep. Nadira was one of those people who, if she woke up before she wanted to, found it impossible to fall asleep again.

So instead of lying there she got up and put on a fresh pot of coffee. She sat on one of the barstools next to her breakfast nook to sip the hot brew wistfully, wishing she was staring out of her grandmother's kitchen window.

That was a sight... five acres of open land with the oak tree up on the hill. She recalled waking up as a child and running out barefoot to watch the sun rise, feeling the dew on the grass underneath her feet. She would come back in to find her grandmother's fresh biscuits on the table with a jar of molasses ready to spread.

Those were days that built her into the woman she was today. Her sisters might not have appreciated what Gran had offered, but she did. A touch of sadness came to the surface thinking about her sisters who wanted the high life. They had all been graced with the talent of music. But the call of hip-hop stars and watching the music channel had put stars in their eyes from a young age. They rebelled against their grandmother. Thanks to her mother, she had learned from an early age you can't stop the runaway train when it's barreling down the tracks. *And we Webbs are stubborn when we get on a mission.*

She decided after breakfast she would head out to the two-story homestead and work. Just thinking about it made her want to move in all the more. Nadira intended to be moved in by the end of spring so she could spend summer nights sitting on the back porch.

It was way better than looking out into the parking lot of her complex. An hour later, with a waffle in her mouth, she got in her car and headed in the familiar direction of home. Last night Steve had picked her up for the military ball, and when he saw she would be staying he went home.

The part of last night that she tried hard not to think about was Logan. Every time his face popped into her memory the heat of their lovemaking and the intensity of their connection made her tingle and scared as hell.

"Okay, you will not think of Logan Ross, or his sexy eyes, or the way he kisses you, or how his hands..."

She shook her head trying to escape the heat that flamed in her body. She wasn't going to say no to dating Logan, that's for sure, but she would make sure to keep her heart protected and not in the line of fire.

Her grandmother's house came into view. The new, white paint gleamed in the sunlight, beckoning her. She made sure the outside work was done way before the winter chill had come in. February in Kansas had no snow on the ground, but it was cold as heck, and she certainly preferred to be working inside rather than out.

When she went inside the smell of new paint and freshly varnished hardwood floors filled her nostrils, and happiness filled her chest as she began to work. When all the renovations were complete, by summer she would be giving piano lessons in that living room with the big bay window and the sun streaming through.

It was well into the afternoon before she looked up from the mantle piece she was stripping of paint, trying to get back to the original wood beneath. A knock sounded and she frowned, not expecting anyone. Nadira went to the door, wiping her hands before peeking through the keyhole. Logan was standing on the other side. She took a calming breath and opened the front door but left the second screened door a locked barrier between them.

"Well, how did you find me, soldier?" Nadira asked casually.

"I'm a man of great secrets and means," Logan announced grandly.

"In other words, you went online and looked up my grandmother's address?" Nadira surmised.

Logan gave her a boyish grin. "Yeah, but my way made me sound more mysterious."

Nadira couldn't help but laugh. "Why should I let you in, Major?"

He held up a picnic basket. "I come bearing the gift of lunch."

Nadira pretended to consider before she unlocked the screen door and held it open for him to enter. "You're lucky I only had a waffle for breakfast."

"So you want me only for my food?" Logan asked.

"Maybe."

He put the basket down and pulled her into his arms. "Well, I want something more."

Her eyes closed of their own accord when his lips touched hers, and the kiss they shared made her begin to smolder.

"Hey, sexy lady, I missed you," he said softly when he raised his head.

"You saw me only a few hours ago." Nadira licked her lips, enjoying the taste of him.

"Doesn't matter."

"How can you be so sure about me, about this, like it's out of your hands?" she asked incredulously.

"Because everything lined up so perfectly. How could I not?" He cupped her cheek and looked at her with such tenderness Nadira felt overwhelmed. "You said your grandmother had the gift. Why can't you open your heart to believe we were meant to meet at this time?"

She shook her head in refusal. "Because, I've seen how loving a man so much can make you forget your kids, your life, and even your soul. I can't give myself over to someone that much."

"I'll change your mind with my irresistible charm," Logan said. He pulled away and looked around the big living room, effectively changing the subject. "You have a nice space here. We'll eat lunch, and I'll roll up my sleeves and help."

"Don't you have soldiering or marching to do?" Nadira asked.

"Honey, we just came back from a nine month tour. We get a few weeks off." His grin was disarming. He pulled a red checkered tablecloth from the top of the basket and spread it on the floor before sitting. "Come see what I brought for lunch."

Nadira sat and took off her beat up sneakers before scooting close to peek in the basket. "Nine months, where was your unit stationed?"

"We were in Kandahar," Logan answered. "Glad to be home, though. A few of our guys got hurt. Some didn't make it back, but we got through it and came home. That's why the Valentine's Day ball was so important for them, to reaffirm that they were back safe with their families."

As light and easy as his voice was, Nadira noted how tense his shoulders became and the way he swallowed with even one small mention of the men they lost. Her grandmother's home was close enough to Fort Leavenworth that she had seen soldiers all her life. This was something new to her, and she guessed for a lot of people and families. Dealing with the aftereffects and seeing guys coming back from the front lines with scars both inside and out.

"How about you, Logan? What reaffirms life for you?" Nadira asked softly.

He gave her a slow smile, but his eyes spoke volumes. "I think I found mine."

She had no doubt what he meant but avoided going further. *I don't know if I could handle...* She let the thought end there. "So what's in the basket, soldier boy?"

He rubbed his hands together. "Look at the feast I have for you, sweetheart. Fresh fruit, hot paninies, fresh salad with a nice vinaigrette, and fried chicken."

Nadira laughed. "Fried chicken somehow seems like it does not fit."

He gave her a sheepish look that was entirely cute. "That was one of the things I was craving in Kandahar. Friend chicken from Belle's Place. I still haven't had enough."

"Do you mind if I get a piece too, or is it all for you?" she teased.

Logan clasped his hands over his heart. "I don't know if I wanna share."

"Share with me, and the favor will be repaid." Nadira lowered her voice to a sexy purr.

"Stop that. If not, we won't be eating lunch," he responded.

"It meant that you'll go home and get changed and come over for dinner." She laughed. "Trust me. Very few get to enjoy my fabulous cooking."

"I'll take that deal."

The comfortable conversation went on as they ate lunch. After they cleaned up the remnants and threw what they could in the big trash bin she kept handy,

Logan took over stripping the mantle, commenting on how cool it would look with a fire roaring inside it by next winter. She was thinking the same thing and just smiled as she stained the wood banister heading up the stairs.

"I'll do the varnishing for you tomorrow."

She was so busy in her task that she didn't know he came up behind her until he wrapped his hands around her and lifted her from the bottom step. Nadira squealed as her back was pressed against his chest. For a moment she let go and relaxed, luxuriating in the feel of his warmth and the hardness of his body.

"I can't let you do all my work. That's not fair. You've only been home for a few weeks. You should be relaxing," she murmured.

He kissed her temple, and she felt his breath against her skin as he spoke. "Honey, my finger is not on the trigger of a gun, and I'm not in a place where every car or even a donkey could be strapped with something to kill me as I pass by. I want to help. This is my way of de-stressing."

She nodded. "I guess I can't stop you, huh?"

"Not unless you have some rope lying around." He gave her a slow grin. "Hey, that might be fun."

She slapped at his chest. "Your mind is in the gutter."

"Never." He pulled her close for a gentle kiss. "I plan to share this fireplace with you eventually."

"Go get cleaned up. I'll meet you at my place."

He raised an eyebrow at her in amusement. They both knew she was avoiding his last statement. "You are as obvious as a Mack truck."

She smiled. "True, but at least you always know where I'm coming from."

"Around five?" he asked before kissing her good-bye.

"Make it six. I need to make a stop at the grocery store," Nadira explained.

"See you then."

She watched Logan leave and sighed. Nadira wished for a moment that she was one of those women who could see the prospect of falling in love with some sense of innocent delight. Instead, she always looked ahead to when it would end and built herself up for the good-bye.

Most of the time it was her who did the leaving, but this time she knew she wouldn't walk out of this one unscathed like she always did. She asked herself the obvious question. *Then why aren't you stopping it?* The answer was that she couldn't even if she wanted to.

Chapter Three

Logan was antsy way before six, so by five he was out the door. There was actually nothing to do on base. Most of the men and women who came home were with their families. It was a completely different situation from when being in theater, or as civilians called it, deployed.

Over there everyone was in the same situation, and they learned to depend on each other through good times when the FOBs, "forward operations base," were relaxed, and the bad times when they went out on patrols or in convoys or through an attack. They were brothers and sisters in arms. They fought, lived, and died together.

But back home, even though the camaraderie of the unit was still there, each person focused on their families and the people they left behind. Logan had no one to focus on, and usually that meant he would go take a trip and forget military life for awhile. He could always find someone to share his bed. But he was not that type of guy.

There were too many of them on base who wanted to be the playboys out on the town collecting women. Now there was Nadira, and instinct told him she was the one. Before he pulled up outside her apartment, Logan stopped for flowers. The shop door dinged merrily, and he bit back a groan when he saw the woman behind the counter. It couldn't be helped that he dated Michelle months before.

But she was the type whose sweet face belied the nasty personality behind it. She hid it well from the world, but he learned firsthand about her conniving ways. Needless to say, when he told her goodbye she was not the happiest person. He wished he could turn right around, but the flower shop she co-owned was the closest thing he could find. He just hoped it was her timid business partner Susan that would be there, but no such luck.

"Why Logan Ross, you grace my door." Michelle smiled widely. "What can I do for you? I assume dinner. Well, I can't close the shop until seven."

"That's not happening, Michelle, and you know it," Logan replied blandly. "I'm here as a customer, nothing more. I need a mix of those white and pink orchids over there."

"Hot date?" Restrained anger filled her tone.

"None of your business," Logan snapped and then sighed. "You know what, never mind. I'll go somewhere else."

Michelle stopped him. "No, you're absolutely right. It's none of my business. I just wasted five months of my life, that's all. I'll get your bouquet for the lucky woman who caught your eye."

"How much?" he asked pulling out his wallet.

"Nothing at all. Call it a gift." Michelle's saccharine smile didn't faze him.

"No, thank you. How much for the flowers?" Logan wanted nothing she offered for free.

"Fine. Thirty-five dollars." The frozen fake smile on her face never moved.

He knew she overcharged him, but he put two twenties on the counter before plucking the bouquet from her fingers. "Keep the change."

He walked out without another word, all the while feeling her angry stare focused on his back. *What was I thinking dating her?* he wondered as he got into his truck and pulled out of the parking spot. He turned his attention on seeing Nadira again. His need to see her was fierce, even though they had spent the entire afternoon together.

The little blue Saturn she drove was already parked there, and he jumped out of his truck taking the flowers off the passenger seat as he moved. Logan knew his steps were hurried as he headed up the stairs, but the urge to see her again was a longing that would not be denied. It almost frightened him with its intensity. From the first touch, he knew that she was his.

Nadira opened the door on the first knock, and he stared at her for what seemed like endless moments. She left him tongue-tied. Her dark hair cascaded down her back and shoulders. Her ebony skin had a satiny sheen that captured the light. She wore a midnight blue dress that stopped mid-thigh and silk stocking that covered her long legs.

His gaze trailed back up her body. Logan was definitely not thinking about dinner when he met her warm brown eyes or the smile that graced her full lips. He wondered vaguely if she would mind him lifting her and making his way toward her bed.

"Dinner first." Her smile widened as if she read his mind. Nadira stepped back to allow him to enter.

Logan kissed her lightly. "I was thinking about dinner."

"I'm sure you were, and I was on the menu," she teased.

"Do you blame me? You look absolutely amazing." Logan sniffed the air appreciatively. "It smells good in here."

"Thank you. I made a seafood linguini with a creamy wine sauce, homemade garlic bread, and a merlot is ready to be poured," Nadira replied and plucked the flowers from his hand. "I take it these are for me?"

Logan laughed when she crossed behind the counter into the small kitchen area. "What can I say? You make me forget everything but you."

She pulled a vase from under the sink and filled it with water. "Do these lines work on all the girls?"

He moved so he stood on the other side of the counter. His tone was serious when he spoke. "No other girls, only you."

"I wish you wouldn't say things like that. We're just barely getting to know each other," she replied. "I don't expect anything from you."

"You should. I want you to be mine, Nadira. The thought of any other man trying to make a play for you would make me hit him," Logan said honestly. "When are you going to believe that we were meant for each other? Hell, I left your house a few hours ago and was antsy to get back and see you again. No other woman has made me want to get closer to her like you have."

She ducked her head, and he saw the shy smile on her face. He knew she wanted to hide it, because from what he'd seen of Nadira, she never showed vulnerability in front of anyone. Her voice was always sweet and melodic, down to the husky laugh that sent shivers along his back. But the cool facade that said nothing ever fazed her was her security blanket.

Logan grinned, knowing he was affecting her after all. He poured two glasses of wine and handed her one over the counter. She touched the petals of the orchids one last time before taking the wine.

She came around the counter. "We have a little bit of time before dinner is ready. The mussels need to steam."

He followed her over to the sofa. "Where did you learn to cook like that?"

"It's one of my favorite things to do other than play the piano," Nadira admitted, and then sighed wistfully. "It's not the same here, though. In the remodeled kitchen at my grandmother's house, I have the view of the back yard and the herb gardens out there. I can see straight up to the big oak tree."

"You keep calling it your grandmother's house," Logan said before taking a sip of wine. "Seems to me with all the renovations you are making, you've made it your own."

She gave a soft laugh. "I've been trying to think of it that way, but she is the one who gave me the happy memories there. Sometimes I feel like I would be disrespecting her if I said it was mine even though she left it to me."

Logan took her hand. "The memories will still be there even if you call it your house. In a way, I wish I had that problem."

"Well, Major Ross, you know my story. What's yours?" Nadira asked.

He shrugged. "There's nothing much to tell. I grew up in foster care, got kicked out of it when I was eighteen, no place to go, so the army became my home. It's been that way for nineteen years."

"I'm sorry, Logan." She squeezed his hand.

"Why? I'm not. I've had a good life in the military. I've always wanted something more, a family, to be a father, to spend the rest of my life with someone."

"Don't say..." she began to protest.

He cupped her cheek and turned her averted face to his. "No, I'm going to say it, Nadira. I swear to all that's holy in this world I've found that in you."

"It's too soon to say that." Nadira's tone was almost pleading.

"Whirlwind relationships happen," Logan pointed out. "I know a commander who is retired now. He met his wife right after Pearl Harbor. They got married in a week, and fifty years later they are still together. Tell me that isn't something amazing. Who doesn't want that in their lives?"

"Not every relationship works out that way," she said.

"You've seen the worst of what love has to offer. Let me show you how good it can be." Logan pulled her close and repeated, "Let me show you."

Logan kissed her, and to him, the world tipped on its axis. Nothing felt so right as heat traveled to his groin and hardened his cock. Without breaking their lip lock, he stood and lifted her into his arms.

"Where's your bedroom?" he asked.

"The first door on the right," she replied. "Logan, the mussels. Dinner will be ruined."

He made a beeline to the stove and flicked the knob to off with her still in her arms before heading to the bedroom. "I don't mind cold pasta. All I want is you."

The bedroom was not decorated the way he would expect a woman's room to be. In fact, as he put her on her feet he only noticed one photo on the bedside table. Logan knew it was probably because she wanted to put it all back into the childhood home she loved, so this place was not a home. The big ornate huge mahogany bed was the only thing that dominated the room. He looked at it with a raised eyebrow.

"It was my first big purchase when I really got my musical career off the ground. It's a bitch to take apart and put together, but I sleep best on this bed," she said with a smile.

"Let's test it out," Logan murmured.

His lips descended on hers once again, and the taste of her wiped everything else out of his mind. She pressed herself closer to him, and Logan loved the feel of her against him. With hands reaching and caressing each other while they undressed, Logan trailed kisses down her torso. He reached the tops of her silky stockings and moaned against the soft skin of her stomach when he found she wore nothing above them.

"Oh hell, you are trying to kill me." He looked up at her. "All this time while we talked you weren't wearing panties?" he asked huskily.

"I thought it would be a nice surprise when it was finally revealed." He could hear the arousal in her voice.

"If I had known, I'd probably have taken you on the sofa." Logan shuddered thinking about taking her.

He took each stocking from the garter belt and threw them on the bed before taking that off as well.

She stood naked in front of him, and he was inches away from her pussy. The call to taste her was undeniable. He kissed her mound, and she gasped.

Logan slipped his tongue between her pussy lips, and she cried out. Her taste was intoxicating, something exotic and sexy that he couldn't get enough of. She spread her legs to give him more access. With a loud groan he bent lower and loved her with his lips and tongue. He teased her with one little flick of his tongue against her clit.

"I don't think I can stand this. My legs feel so weak."

He looked up at her, and she was holding onto one of the carved mahogany posts of the canopy bed. He wanted her to trust him in all things and decided to see how willing she was to let go for a little while.

"I'm going to make you come, and you won't fall. Don't let go of the bed no matter what, understand?" Logan asked gruffly. The thought of what he was about to do made his cock so hard it ached.

"Yes." Her breath was coming in short little pants of excitement.

Logan positioned her so she was still standing, but the back of her thighs were against the bed. He spread her legs wider, and without another word, he tasted her again. Her flavor drove him wild, and with a savage groan he cupped her ass and penetrated her with his tongue then sucked her on the bud of her clit.

"Oh my God!" she screamed.

Logan moaned in response. It was primal to his own ears. The carnal need to take her to the edge was great. Her hips undulated against his mouth while she panted and begged for more. "Yes, yes please, Logan, now!" she moaned. Her body arched, and she came with a gasping cry. He licked as her juices flowed, and his groans of delight filled the room. His breath was labored when he moved from between her legs. It was not from exertion but from trying to hold on tight to the last threads of sanity that kept him from taking her like an animal.

"I want you, I want you." She said the words in a chant. He took her lips, and he felt her nails in his back.

He pulled away, expelling a huge breath. "Wait, oh goddamn! When I touch you, it's like driving a fast car, zero to sixty in seconds, and I want this to last."

"You can have more anytime. Take me," she encouraged him. Nadira sat back on the bed and spread her legs. "Take what's yours."

Logan regained his composure and sat next to her on the bed. "Oh, baby, I am glad to hear you say that, but this will happen in my time. Do you trust me?"

She met his gaze. "Yes, no, I don't know."

"I'm asking you to trust me."

Logan lifted her as if she weighed nothing and settled her back on the pillows at the head of the bed. He picked up the discarded stockings from where he threw them and glided the silky material through his hands. Nadira followed his movements until she looked at him with wide eyes.

"Will you give yourself over to me?" It was the ultimate question of trust, and Logan knew by asking it, he was taking a big step.

She licked her lips and gave him a nod. "Yes, I will."

Taking one stocking he folded it in two before wrapping it around her wrist in a soft loop and then tying her arm to the bed. He trailed the other stocking across her skin before doing the same to the other hand. She was bound against the bed, unable to move and under his control. He pressed a hot kiss on her breasts, taking her nipple into his mouth.

Nadira cried out, sat up, and pulled against the restraints around her wrists. Logan kissed her into submission and ceased her struggles against her bonds. He used his body weight to press her back into the bed. His fingers trailed down her body to where he played between the wet folds of flesh, up and down in slow, deliberate movements.

His tongue penetrated her mouth while he barely rubbed his fingers over her clit before circling the entrance of her snatch. Her body shivered again under his control, and it made him feel like he could conquer the world because she succumbed to his touch. She tried to move her body to let his fingers bury deep inside her. *Not yet,* he thought and continued to tease the sensitive outer flesh.

"Please," Nadira whispered. Her head tossed restlessly on the bed.

"Please what?" Logan prompted. He wanted her to ask for what she wanted.

"Your fingers, put them inside me, Logan." She arched and spread her legs wider.

"Look at me," he ordered. "I want to see the pleasure in your eyes."

Her eyes snapped open, and he met the liquid chocolate brown eyes with his gaze. His finger slid into her slick opening, so very slowly until he had it buried.

"Oh God, yes!"

He moved his finger and rubbed her clit with his thumb. Nadira's eyes widened, and her lips parted while he watched her. He didn't know which excited him more, watching sensations play on her face, or the feeling of her pussy clutching at his finger.

He kept that slow pace until she begged. "Harder, faster, I need more!"

"You are so responsive. I like that," he murmured. "It's all for me, isn't it? Say it, baby."

"For you, Logan, all for you."

He was just as excited at her response. He slid two fingers deeper, faster, and her head fell back in ecstasy as he played with her. Her hips met his hand in a rhythm that increased to a frenzied pace. Little moans escaped her lips, and he knew she was reaching for her orgasm. He sent his fingers deeper, finding the spot that would send her over the edge.

"Dirty little girl, you're going to come for me now, aren't you?"

"Oooh yes, I'm going to come."

Her hips pushed against his fingers as her body reached that pinnacle. He held his breath as her body drew tight like a bow, and she screamed as the point of her release took her breath. His fingers and hand were dripping with her juices, and she slumped back against the bed.

Logan settled between her legs and rubbed his cock up and down from her ass to her wet pussy slit. He grabbed her curvaceous hips and rammed his cock deep into her center. The loud groan that he emitted when he felt her pussy encase him like a glove mingled with hers.

"God, you feel so good, I won't be able to hold back," Logan told her.

Nadira looked at him. "Don't try. Let go. I want it all."

His control snapped when she raised her legs high even though her arms were suspended above her. This was not the sensual torture from before. He knew it was leading up to one thing, pure, hot, dirty fucking. They came together with raw guttural cries.

Logan heard the sound their bodies made, wet smacking noises every time he thrust into her. She chanted "fuck me" over and over again as he took her. Her orgasms came one after the other like the firestorm they created. He could feel each one clutch and draw at his cock until he could hardly stand it.

His balls tightened, and still he pounded into her pussy that was so wet it ran down her thighs. Without even losing pace, he slipped from her pussy into her tight ass already coated with her come.

"This is how you want it, rough and hard... Tell me this is how you want it!"

"Yes, this is how I want it. Come with me, Logan. I can't stop it!"

He listened to her begging for his seed, for him to fall over into the abyss with her. The plea pushed him over, and with a growl his body released. A harsh roar escaped his lips once, then again as he still pumped inside her. With each thrust, he filled her with his come.

Logan couldn't help when his body fell against hers, and for a moment they laid still trying to catch their breath. He untied her hands and pulled her to him. He held her head cradled against his shoulder, and he couldn't help but press kisses against her temple and then her hand that lay on his chest.

"That was something." She sighed. "Holy hell that was something."

"I'm sorry but the brain you are talking to is offline at the moment. Please leave a message at the beep," Logan murmured. "Beep."

Nadira laughed. "You are insane."

Logan rolled and kissed her. "Crazy for you, doll face. God, I can't believe I have you in my life. I must have done something really good. Thank you."

She looked up at him. "Why are you thanking me?"

"You've given me a future to look forward to."

I should make you some dinner in a little while," she murmured. "After I regain the use of my legs, of course."

Logan noticed that she deftly changed the subject to something in her comfort zone. Any thought of anything serious, she hid like a scared bunny. *One step forward, two steps back*. But it didn't matter. He would have enough faith for both of them.

Chapter Four

Nadira walked down the street after having lunch with Logan. He took off to her house with a load of supplies she needed to continue with the renovations. With his help she had gotten all the floors done and the stairs. The master bedroom had been painted, and the new appliances were already in the kitchen.

By Valentine's Day she would be able to move in and get her stuff out of storage. *Finally!* Valentine's Day was two days away, and her relationship with Logan was exactly what he called it—a whirlwind. She had never known a more enigmatic man in her life. Full of confidence regardless of if he was in uniform, and certainly while he was out of it.

Her mind went back to the lovemaking the night she invited him over to dinner. The meal was a few hours late because he turned her bones to mush. She smiled, remembering how they ate the rich food and drank the wine naked in bed. She was trying hard not to feel anything for Logan, but how could she not?

His confidence scared her most of all, because while he felt they were destined to be together, she had spent her life fighting against fate. He was none too happy that by one in the morning she was asking him to leave. But he respected her wishes and her rules. She wasn't ready to let him breach that barrier.

Now she walked down the street to run a few errands before she took her car back over to the house. She had come from the bakery with a sweet, after-dinner treat for them both. She was putting her wallet in her pocket when a figure blocked her path.

Nadira smiled. "Excuse me. I wasn't looking where I was going."

"You weren't looking at whose man you took either," the woman snapped back.

Nadira's smile instantly faded. "And who might that be?"

"I saw you having lunch with Logan. You're just his latest fling, and he'll come back to me."

Nadira looked at the woman who had a sneer on her face and felt instant dislike. Logan may have dated her, and it ended badly. The woman probably thought if she confronted her, it would make some kind of problem. Nadira was not that kind of person, and she looked this lady up and down.

"And you might be?" Nadira asked.

"Michelle. I own the flower shop. He came in and bought flowers, so I knew he had a trick."

Oh no she didn't! Nadira certainly didn't want a confrontation on the streets, but no one talked down to her. "Oh, sweetie, it must have felt like crap to have a man who you're drooling over come in and buy flowers for me. Obviously you weren't that important."

Anger flared in Michelle's eyes. "You bitch. You think you can keep him? Let me tell you, he's had quite a few women in this town. You aren't the first, and you sure as hell won't be the last."

"Let me ask you something. Michelle, is it? The name really isn't memorable, after all." Nadira smiled coldly. "Anyway, do I look like the kind of woman who listens to this crap? Go try your scratchy kitty play on someone else. I'm not buying it. Grow up."

Michelle grabbed her hand when she tried to walk away. Nadira looked down at the hand unbelievingly.

"You don't get to walk away from me." Michelle seethed.

The temper that Nadira held onto tightly began to fray. She gave the woman a cold look. "I'm seriously trying to be civil here and not take this to a level you don't want. I will say this. Take your hand off me now, before you lose it. With all these people around, I will be justified in breaking your arm, and trust me. I can."

Nadira smiled sweetly while she looked at the woman. But she hoped that Michelle could see the deadly seriousness in her eyes. Obviously, it gave Michelle thought, and she removed her hand before walking into the bakery in a huff. Nadira went on her way and continued her errands.

She couldn't help that Michelle's words echoed back. If she was one of many women, it would be fine, but why would Logan act like she was the rare gem he was looking for all the time? She had these thoughts and more when she got in to her car to drive to the house. As she unlocked the door, he met her and swept her up in an embrace, dropping kisses all over her lips and face.

Nadira laughed. "Down, boy, down!"

Logan stepped back and pretended to pant. "Fine, but I reserve the right to do it again later."

"We'll see." She passed by with the bakery bag. His eyes watched her shrewdly, and as she guessed, he caught on to her aloofness.

"What's wrong? What happened?"

"I met your ex, Michelle. Or is she one of the women you keep stringing along?" Nadira was surprised to hear the sting in her voice. "Because I don't want to be one of them and sleep with a guy who is sleeping with other women. You need to let me know because..."

"Whoa, Michelle said something to you?" Logan exclaimed. He took her hand and turned her rigid body to his. "Okay, first off, Michelle is a bitch."

"I gathered that," Nadira said stiffly.

Logan grinned. "Second, I broke up with her before I left for Afghanistan. I kinda figured something was wrong when she wanted me to marry her or give her my power of attorney just in case I didn't come back."

"You're kidding!" Nadira exclaimed. "I should've kicked her ass for that alone."

"You don't need to soil your hands on her, and no, you are not in a string of women. She just wanted to get you riled up."

Nadira admitted grudgingly, "Well, she did that, but when she tried to stop me from leaving, I was going to slap her senseless."

"You're jealous!" Logan grinned and scooped her up in his arms.

"No, I'm not," Nadira denied.

"Yes, you are, and it's great 'cause that proves you feel something for me." Logan kissed her soundly.

"I never said I don't feel something." She slapped at his shoulder. "Now quit that. If not, I'm not sharing dessert."

"You don't share dessert, you don't get your present," he said solemnly.

"What present?"

He put his hand over her eyes, and they clumsily went up the stairs. When she opened her eyes, she saw her huge bed was in the middle of the master bedroom with the two matching bedside tables. She squealed and jumped up and down before turning to give him a huge hug and a kiss.

"When did you do this? You didn't have that much of a head start!" she exclaimed.

"I kind of lifted your keys for the apartment and had a few of the guys on base get it over here," Logan admitted. "Everything is almost done downstairs, and I don't see why you can't move in sooner. I checked the heater and turned it on so you can have heat, and I even made sure you have hot water for your first bath."

"Oh my God, you luscious man, you. I need to run back out and get shower curtains and some towels from the apartment," she said. It was unbelievable that he had done this for her.

"Already done."

He opened the bathroom door that adjoined the master bedroom, and she saw the candle lit and the rich red shower curtain he put up to match the bathroom mats he also seemed to have picked up.

"You did all this for me." Her voice held amazement and took on a wispy tone, and tears threatened. He knew she wanted to be home, and he gave her something that meant more than any material gift he could buy.

He shrugged. "I knew it would mean a lot to you."

She did the one thing she said she would never do. Nadira reached up and kissed him. "Stay the night with me, Logan."

He shook his head. "You don't have to do that just because you think you owe me something."

"No, I want you to, because I want to sleep next to you tonight," she answered honestly.

He smiled and pulled her close. "Then I'll stay."

"Wanna test out my new bed?" Nadira invited in a sultry tone.

The look on his face was one of amusement. "Technically, I have tested it out, and it's not new."

"Potato, Po-ta-toe," she replied. She wound her arms around his neck. "It's new for here. You will be the first guest I have in my home."

"I'll be your only male guest," Logan growled before nuzzling her neck. He looked at her again. "You don't have to sleep with me, you know. If you still have doubts about Michelle and her venom, it would be best if I leave."

Nadira shook her head in denial. She didn't have doubts about him being truthful, and his words just proved it. He was honorable and as true blue as they come. "I trust you, Logan."

He kissed her slow and deep while moving toward the bed. Nadira drank in his taste. It intoxicated her, and it felt like she could never get enough. Their kiss deepened. She nibbled and nipped at his lips, then soothed them with her tongue. She did this until the teasing drove him wild, and he buried his hands in her hair.

He took her mouth, ravishing it like a man dying of thirst. It amazed her, his unbridled ferocity when it came to lovemaking. It left her breathless and wanting, craving his touch. She felt as if she could get drunk off his kisses. Her hands roved across his back to his neck and face.

Nadira loved the feel and contours of his body. Logan lifted her, and she wrapped her legs around his waist. They became lost in their passion. He sat on the bed while their tongues dueled, but he suddenly pulled away to look at her.

"Surrender to me, Nadira. I don't just want your body. I want all of you." Logan's voice was husky and filled with emotion. "I've fallen in love with you."

"I-I don't know," she stammered.

He cupped her cheek. "Don't you feel something for me? Anything?"

"I do, Logan. God knows I do, but I can't..." She shook her head. "The words are hard to say. It feels completely scary."

"Try for me. I want to give you my love. I want yours in return."

They undressed slowly, placing a kiss on any patch of skin they could find. Logan lifted her into his arms and sat on the bed again. This time her wet pussy was pressed against him, and she could feel the hardness of his cock. *I want him inside me so bad.*

The thought rushed through her head, fueling her need. This was a different kind of lovemaking. She felt the intensity but something more. It was his love with each touch. His fingers caressed down her back, across the firm line of her buttocks, and to her thighs.

She pulled him closer, and his body shuddered at her touch. He broke the kiss and teased her like she had teased him minutes before, biting her lips then soothing them with his tongue. She ground her body against his waiting cock. He moaned in the back of his throat, telling her that he was being affected the same way.

"More," she whispered. "Please, give me more."

"Will you give me all of you? I want your mind, body, and soul to be mine. Jesus, Nadira, I want you to love me," Logan asked.

"You have me," she replied.

"Let go of those walls you put up whenever the conversation gets serious. I won't ever hurt you. I promise you here and now."

She believed him. God knows she trusted every word he said. But her heart was the last thing she could hold onto under lock and key. *Can I give it to him?*

"There's no one else but you. No other woman has made me feel this way. You're my every thought and dream, my forever," he whispered. "I love you."

She lifted her forehead and looked at him, and tears slipped down her ebony cheeks. He kissed them away, whispering words of love, and Nadira's last walls crumbled and fell. She whispered the words foreign to her lips. "I love you." She had never said them to another soul. As she said it, it felt completely and utterly right. "I love you, Logan."

He took her breath away with the passion that flowed from him at that moment when all her fear ebbed into nothingness. Logan held her tight as his mouth plundered her. Her tongue twisted and turned in his mouth, a seductive dance that he joined willingly. Nadira slipped her hand between their bodies and took his hard cock in her grasp.

She stroked him, and Logan's body surged in pleasure, pressing more intimately against her smooth palm. She lifted her body just enough that she could take him in, sliding his cock into her warm waiting pussy. A groan escaped from his lips when he sank into her wetness.

"God, you feel so good. I want to savor you wrapped around my cock," he whispered.

Nadira had other plans. Her body writhed against him slowly, sending his cock deeper inside her. She couldn't help the little moans that escaped her lips.

His big, strong hands massaged the firm globes of her breasts, and he took each nipple into his mouth while she rode him.

Pleasure infused her core, and she pumped against him faster taking his hard rod deeper within the depths of her sex. Her hands kneaded his back, and his fingers tangled in her hair.

"Do you like how it feels to be inside me, filling me with your cock?" she asked.

"Fuck, yes, baby," he growled in response.

Nadira could hardly bear the sensations tumbling through her. "More." The one word was ripped from his lips before he turned the tables and flipped her so she was on her back. Without missing a move he thrust and at the same time he moved her higher on the bed. Nadira cried out as he pumped into her ferocious with his need. He groaned, and she arched and gasped in pleasure.

His lips and hands were everywhere touching and tasting. He became ravenous in his taking of her. To her it seemed as if he couldn't get enough of her taste, her smell. She was thrown into ecstasy with each movement of his cock inside her. His guttural moans filled the air before he bit her neck. She shivered and raised her hips higher, and the beginning of her orgasm took hold.

"Oh God, I'm coming!" She dug her fingers into his back, feeling as if she had to hold on for dear life.

Logan kissed her hand and said, "Feel me, how much I want you, how much I need you, always. God, I love you so much!"

Nadira gave in to the pleasure, and her orgasm rocked her to her very core. Her body bucked under him, and her pussy gushed, overflowing with her juices. Logan followed suit, and with a harsh cry of her name, his body strained above hers as he emptied his seed within her pussy. His back was slick as she caressed him. She could feel her heartbeat return to its normal rhythm when he levered off her and lay on his back. She missed his weight and snuggled close, throwing a naked thigh across his lower body.

"You said you love me." His chest moved with laughter. "I've found you, and I love you more than you will ever know."

"Mmmhmm," Nadira murmured.

Her mind worked frantically now that the clouds of passion had been erased. She did love him. She knew she could never take it back. But fear etched its way in her heart. She would lose herself now, be consumed by him and his love until she couldn't remember who she was. As his fingers trailed against the skin of her shoulder and he murmured endearments while he held her tight, terror filled her entire being.

Chapter Five

Valentine's night, and he sat in the restaurant waiting for Nadira. Logan's hand went nervously to his pocket where a box was nestled since he bought it. He hadn't seen her since the night when they declared their love for each other. She was busy moving things into her new place, and she had an event out of town with the band.

He didn't even know how popular she was until he had Googled her name and found she was an up and coming jazz singer, with piano solos and events all over the country under her belt. He bought some of the CDs, and when he was on base, her sexy, smoky voice crooned to him and made him yearn for her all the more.

More than once fellow soldiers asked what he was listening to. He had no problem telling them that the voice they heard was his wife to be. Logan had to admit he was in a daze since that night. The day seemed brighter each morning when he woke up. He got his new orders on base. One more week of leave, and then he would be in his new office as the head intelligence officer on the base. He couldn't wait to tell her there would be no more deployments and that he wanted to share his life with her.

He felt like a complete goof sometimes. Being in love made him feel kind of crazy. But he'd been searching for the right one for a long time, and he had found her. He fingered the box in his pocket again, anxious for her to come in. The nervous twitch in his belly was not going away.

The minute she came in, everything around him faded away. The clink of glasses and utensils on china all became muted when his eyes met hers. She was dressed in white. The material sparkled as if she caught the stars, and it hugged her body then flared off to her knees.

He drank her in, from the dangling earrings that sparkled on each ear to the white satin shoes. He stood when the host led her over with a smile. The man gave him a wink when he left, and he was finally alone with her.

"I missed you. Do you know how much I want to kiss you right now?" He was amazed at the hoarseness of his voice.

She smiled. "You saw me two days ago, Logan, but I missed you too."

He walked around to pull out her chair for her and couldn't resist taking one kiss. "Good."

"We could've met at my place and cooked together." Nadira sat and put her purse in her lap.

Logan laughed. "Um, yeah, we end up eating much later anytime we do that. This is Valentine's Day. I wanted to actually let you eat a meal without me ravishing you."

"That is true, so let's see what's on the menu. I'm actually famished." Nadira picked up the thin book from the table.

Logan followed suit. The casual conversation was driving him crazy. The box in his pocket felt like a stone. "How was your trip? Did the crowd go wild?"

"It was amazing. We did two extra sets. I played the new piece that I played for you when we met, and the crowd loved it." Nadira grinned.

The waiter brought over the wine and poured two glasses. Logan waited for him to leave before speaking. "Well, next time I hope I can go with you and see you in action. I think I have turned all the guys on base into your fans as well. I've been playing your CDs constantly."

"I didn't know you even knew I had music out there," she said surprised.

Logan took her hand and smiled. "I knew."

The conversation waned as she took a sip of wine. Logan played with her fingers and let out a long sigh.

"What's wrong?" she asked.

"I can't wait any longer," Logan replied. "I love you, and I want to spend the rest of my life with you, Nadira. This is so right, and all the pieces fit into place so perfectly that I have to see it as destiny putting us together."

He pulled the box from his pocket, and her eyes widened.

"Logan, what are you doing? Please..." She shook her head.

"No, let me finish. Nadira, I got my new assignment today, and I'm going to be stationed here permanently. I want to spend my life with you. Marry me, and I promise you will never regret one moment of it, even fifty years from now," Logan finished with a rush.

He opened the box and showed her the ring. It caught the light, and she gasped, putting her hand to her chest in what he hoped was delight. But when she looked up at him, behind the tears, all he saw was terror. She shook her head, trying to form words, and nothing came out. Nadira got up suddenly and rushed from the restaurant, and he followed amidst the stares in their direction.

He caught up to her easily and turned her around to face him. "I ask you to marry me, and you run? I thought you loved me."

"I-I do, but I can't, Logan. Let me go!" She struggled against him.

"Give me a reason, one reason why you can't process loving me as something good!" he ground out.

"Just let me go, please!" She pulled out of his arms and ran to her car and got in. When she drove off he heard her tires squeal in her haste to get away.

He closed the lid on the engagement ring box, and the snap seemed to echo in the night. Hurt filled his chest along with anger and fury that made him want to hit something. He punched the wall of the restaurant so hard pain radiated up his hand.

He knew he had probably fractured a bone. He looked down the street as the car receded into the night. *I guess I fell in love with the wrong one*, he thought. But in his heart he knew that was far from the truth. *So, this is what a broken heart feels like,* he thought walking back into the restaurant to pay for the wine.

Back at his car he looked up to the full moon that hung low in the sky. *Gypsy moon.* He remembered the story she told him, and he ached all the more. Logan would have preferred the pain of a bullet wound compared to what he felt now.

"OH JESUS, WHAT DID I do? What did I just do!" Nadira cried out and slapped her hand against the steering wheel.

The look on Logan's face was one that she could never forget. *I did that to him,* she thought while tears streamed down her cheeks. She hurt him, and she never wanted to do that to anyone. *Then why aren't you turning around to go beg him to forgive you?* a voice in her mind sneered. But the thought of that filled her with just as much hurt and dread, so she kept driving for hours, not knowing exactly where she was going.

When exhaustion finally began to creep in, she pulled in to a Walmart and bought some stuff, then went across to the hotel that was right next door and checked in. In the room she dropped the bags tiredly on the table and pulled out a pair of sweatpants and a tank shirt she bought. She went into the bathroom and put them on before braiding her hair in a long braid down her back.

She couldn't go home. Logan would find her there and ask for the truth. She looked at her despair-filled eyes in the mirror and wondered what she could tell him. *I'm so jaded that loving you scares me, or should I just say I'm so broken I can't be fixed?*

At that point she hated her mother more than she even thought possible. And the man her mother married who warped her sense of love. She hated a father she never met and sisters who didn't stick around so they could handle it together. She hated her grandmother for dying and leaving her.

She would know what to do. She thought she had handled these issues well enough, but it seemed that was far from the truth. She came out of the bathroom and sat on the bed. Nadira turned the TV on to something mindless that would fill the quiet room and erase her tumultuous thoughts.

When her stomach rumbled, she grabbed a bag of chips and a can of soda from the case of twelve she bought. She sat there refusing to think of Logan or the hurt in his eyes for as long as she could. She managed to keep everything at bay for that night when she fell into an exhausted sleep. By the next day she was awake but lying in bed sobbing her eyes out at what she had done.

More than once she picked up her cell phone and saw that Logan had called numerous times. She went to hit redial, and each time her hand froze over the button, wondering what she should say. That led to another torrent of tears, because she knew he was not the kind of man who would take to having a relationship with no strings attached. He was an all or nothing kind of man, and Logan wanted it all.

By noon she fell asleep again, and this time her dreams gave her the answers. She opened her eyes under the oak tree in the back yard, and the sun through the trees caused her to shade her eyes. She looked over and found her grandmother spreading the tarot cards like she usually did, and she smiled.

"Gran, I'm dreaming, aren't I?" Nadira scrambled up to sit.

"Of course you are, and didn't I tell you that love would find you no matter how you denied it would?" her grandmother said.

"Yes, you did, but now I've hurt Logan, and I don't know what to do." Nadira turned pleading eyes to her grandmother. "I'm so scared. Tell me what to do."

"I certainly can't tell you that. You have to look at your choices. How will you feel if you don't have him in your life?"

"It would feel like a hole in my chest. I do love him, Gran," Nadira answered honestly.

"How would it feel if you have him?" The older lady continued to spread the cards on the checkered blanket without looking up.

"Scared but happy. I feel like I might lose me in the mix like Mom did, but I don't think he would let that happen," Nadira admitted. "He's such a good man. He loves so fiercely I'm afraid."

This time her Gran looked up at smiled. "You answered your own questions then. Work through the fear and see the man who loves you so fiercely. He will never let you lose who you are. Go to him, and he'll forgive you. Love him as much as he loves you."

Nadira nodded. "I do, Gran. I really do. Thank you for helping me."

"This is just a dream, child. Your mind working things out on its own."

Nadira woke with those final words echoing in her mind. For a moment she wondered if it was a dream or her grandmother's way of helping from the beyond. Either way she knew what she had to do. She slipped her feet in the satin shoes she had worn and laughed, knowing she must look a sight dressed in sweats and wearing heels.

She didn't care as she got into the car, and she drove back home as fast as the speed limit would allow. She would go to Logan and apologize, and they would work it out.

By the time she got to the gates of the Fort Leaven-worth military base, she wondered if she should have made a detour and gone home to get cleaned up. *No use worrying about that now*, she thought firmly. She smiled and showed the soldier at the gate her ID and asked for directions to Major Logan Ross's home.

He gave her the information willingly when she ex-plained she was his fiancée. Somehow it seemed that most everyone on base had heard her CDs due to Lo-gan's encouragement. She took a second to sign the front cover of the copy the solider happened to have in the gate house.

She drove the route to base housing, and when she pulled up in front of Logan's house she felt the butter-flies in the pit of her stomach take flight. She pressed her hand against her tummy hoping to relieve the nervous flutter.

Nadira pushed some stray tendrils that had come loose from her braid back in place and zipped the coat of her sweat suit a little higher before pulling it down to make it neat. She knocked on his door and almost thought he was not at home when there was no answer.

She turned to leave when she heard the door unlock from the inside, and he opened the door. He looked at her with hooded eyes that told her nothing. He registered no surprise or emotion at seeing her on his door step. His cheeks carried a five o'clock shadow showing he had not shaved.

This Logan was not the one she knew and loved. He had a hint of hardness about him now, and she noticed the cast that went from his knuckles to his wrist. She heard tendrils of music coming from somewhere in his house and recognized the song was one of hers.

She gave him a nervous smile. "Hey."

He didn't return her greeting. "I called to make sure you were okay. You didn't answer."

"I'm sorry. I had to work through some things," she replied.

"I'm sure you did."

He was not going to make it easier for her, so Nadira rushed right in. "I'm sorry, Logan. So very sorry! I love you. I really do, but the ring scared me with all my mom and my stepfather did when they were married. I thought it would change me, too, that I would forget who I am and become like her."

She took a breath. "It took me driving away to see that you would never let that happen. You would fight for me just because you love me that much!"

She fiddled with her hair before meeting his unchanging gaze once more. "I hurt you. God knows that should be enough for you to never forgive me, but I'm asking you to please give me the chance to erase that hurt, to show you that I will fight for you, too. I'll marry you, Logan, and I am making you the same promise you made me. You will never regret it, because I will love you hard for the rest of your life."

He stood silent, staring at her until she asked nervously, "Aren't you going to say something, anything?"

He didn't say a word. Instead he stepped back inside the door and gave it a little shove. His gaze never left hers, and it swung closed with a click that seemed to say good-bye. She pressed her hand against it, and then her forehead, fighting back the tears.

She slammed a flat palm against the door once then twice as the tears fell. *I've lost him*, she thought numbly, the ache in her heart so fierce that it almost caused her knees to buckle. *No, you haven't. You fight for him!*

She recalled the music she heard when he opened the door. "I'm going to fight for you, Logan Ross. I'm not giving up. I know you still love me, and I'm going to do battle to regain your heart!"

Nadira walked away from the door with determined steps back to her car and drove away. At her house she let the hot tears fall, knowing it was her turn to win the heart of Logan Ross, the one she broke.

Days later she sat at the piano in her house and played desolate notes. Nothing she did got Logan to forgive her, and she had lost hope. Valentine's Day was long gone, and yet she found a way to send him a Valentine's gift via messenger that he promptly returned. He wouldn't take her calls at home or at work. He wouldn't answer the long emails where she poured out her love to him in words. She wrote a new piece of music that she named Gypsy Moon and dedicated to him.

She went to the recording studio and had it put on CD, knowing it would be the centerpiece of her new tracks to be released later in the year. All she really wanted was to teach kids to play in the big room she now sat in. The CDs she made had gained some notoriety, and she was offered a recording contract.

She promptly refused, not changing her goals, but now she didn't have him to share anything with. Her joys and her sorrows would be hers alone. Nadira sent him a copy of her new music with the words, *only you could inspire music like this.* She told him the best way she could through music how much she needed him and missed him, and yet he never replied.

She closed the piano with a frustrated sigh and went upstairs to get dressed for bed. She ached for him, missed his kisses and the way his strong arms held her tight. She missed his grin and the quick funny way he had of making her smile. He loved her until she was breathless and held her through the storm of passion.

Jealousy sickened her to think someone else might have that. She would never have that again with him. Nadira put on her nightgown and opened the window halfway to the night air. It held a chill she hoped would help calm and clear her head. She closed her eyes, and for long hours begged sleep to claim her.

She must have dozed off because she heard soft music coming to her from outside. Confused, she sat up and went to the window. Looking out, she saw no one until a flicker of light caught her gaze from beneath the oak tree. She recognized the music as the piece she wrote for Logan. *Could it be?*

Her heart leapt knowing that only two people had that music, and one was her, so it had to be him. Without a thought she rushed downstairs barefoot and opened the back door. She hesitated a moment, hearing the music louder now she was downstairs. The screen door hinges squeaked as she pushed it open, and it slammed against the wall of the house as she ran.

If the ground was cold under her feet, she didn't feel it. She ran with all her strength toward the man who held her heart. She stopped just before she reached him. He had candles on the ground and a small portable stereo that played her music. He turned to face her, and the candlelight played across his face.

Nadira rushed into his arms, and he held her tight while she kissed him frantically on his cheeks and face before he devoured her mouth. *This is what I needed. Oh God, I missed him!* she thought as they kissed.

She pulled away. "I'm sorry, so sorry, Logan. Please say you'll forgive me."

"Do you love me?" His eyes searched hers.

"I do love you so very much, Major Logan Ross," she replied. "I've been dying these last few weeks without you. You're the other half of me."

"You hurt me something bad, Nadira. I won't deny it. And for a while I thought I could live without you." Logan caressed her mouth with his thumb. "But you kept sending me things, and each of those emails I read and died a little each time without you. The music is what got me. I could feel you in each note. I could picture us every time I played it. I had to come. I love you so damn much. I don't think I could function without you."

"That's hard for a soldier not being able to function," she said with a smile.

He grinned, and she saw the familiar light in his eyes again. "Yeah, especially with a busted hand. I had to lie and tell everyone I fell and fractured it. I couldn't tell them I punched a wall when you drove away."

She kissed the cast. "Oh, baby, I'm going to make it up to you."

"You'd better," he growled and took her lips in a kiss.

"I'll draw hearts all over your cast and write I love you," she whispered.

"Please don't. I have to work with men who will never let me live it down." Logan got to his knees and pulled the ring from his pocket. "You can do this for me. Say yes, Nadira. Marry me."

"A thousand times yes!" she replied as he placed the ring on her finger.

"I wish there was a Gypsy Moon for us to dance under," he murmured.

"We fell in love under one, and that's what counts," Nadira replied. "Hold me tight, Logan, and never let me go."

Their lips met in a kiss that sealed their destiny together, and he held her tight. Nothing felt as right to her as being in his arms, and they swayed to the music she wrote with a love she thought she could never have.

The End

About the Author

Dahlia Rose is the USA Today best-selling multi genre author from Urban fantasy to Romance with a hint of Caribbean spice. She was born and raised on the island of Barbados and now currently lives in Charlotte, North Carolina. Her life revolves around her family and her grandson who she's fondly nicknamed 'the toddler overlord, long may he reign." She has a love of dark fantasy, crazy sci-fi B-movies, and delving into the unknown. Dahlia writes from romance to suspense, giving her characters the voices they deserve, if she doesn't, they surely won't let her sleep. With over seen dozen books published, Dahlia has become a reader favorite. Not only because of her writing but her vivacious attitude in talking to her fans online and at various events. Being a BIPOC, author of color, her books feature strong heroines with a Caribbean or African American culture, that is showcased in the vibrancy of her words. Books and writing are her biggest passions, and she hopes to open your imagination to the beauty of possibilities between the pages of her books.

LinkTree: https://linktr.ee/authordahliarose

Printed in Great Britain
by Amazon